FOR KATHRIN

Don't miss the other books in this series:
THE RAINBOW FISH

First mini-book edition published in the United States, Great Britain,
Canada, Australia, and New Zealand in 2001 by North-South Books,
an imprint of Nord-Süd Verlag AG, Gossau Zürich, Switzerland.
Distributed in the United States by North-South Books Inc., New York.

ISBN 0-7358-1481-3
1 3 5 7 9 10 8 6 4 2
Printed in Belgium

RAINBOW FISH
TO THE RESCUE!
MARCUS PFISTER

TRANSLATED BY J. ALISON JAMES

NORTH-SOUTH BOOKS / NEW YORK / LONDON

A long way out in the deep blue sea there swam a school of fish. Not just ordinary fish— each one had a sparkling silver scale. Ever since Rainbow Fish had shared his scales, these fish had done everything together. They swam together. They played together. They ate together. They even rested together, floating in the shadows of the reef.

They were so happy together, they had no
interest in other fish. So one day, when a little
striped fish swam through their game of flash-
tag, they all stared at him.

"Hey," the little striped fish finally said, "can
I play too?"

"It's flash-tag," said one little fish, "and you
don't have a flashing scale!"

"Do you have to have a special scale?" the little striped fish asked.

"Of course you do!" said the fish with the jagged fins. "Come on, let's play!" he called to the others. "Don't worry about him."

Then all the fish turned and went back to their game.

Rainbow Fish hesitated. He was afraid of losing his new friends, so he didn't dare stand up to the fish with the jagged fins. Feeling a little ashamed, Rainbow Fish reluctantly swam off to join the others.

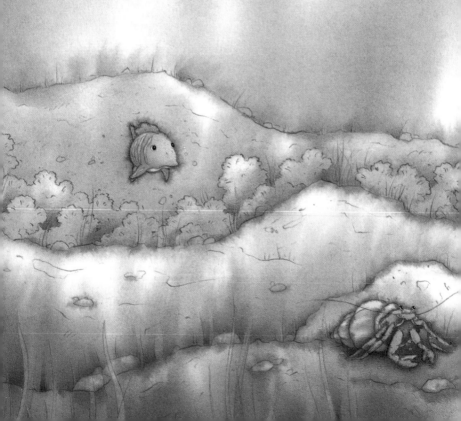

The little striped fish floated all alone at the edge of the reef. He looked sad as he watched the game. The other fish were having such fun—darting and diving in the deep blue sea, their shiny scales sparkling.

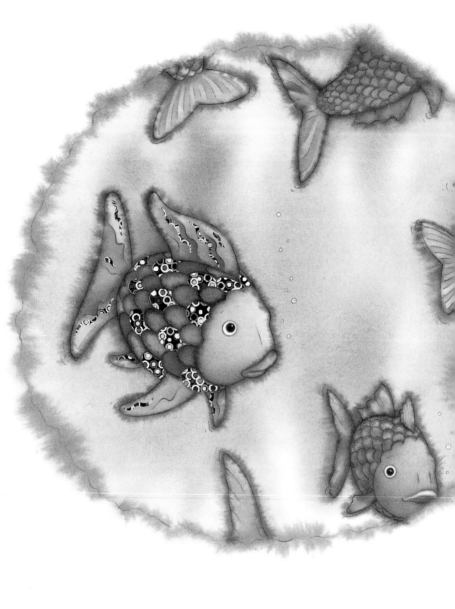

Rainbow Fish remembered what it felt like to have no friends and how lonely he had been when all the fish had ignored *him*. He had been so proud of all his glittering scales that he had refused to share them. No wonder nobody had wanted to play with him.

But now his friends did want him to play, and Rainbow Fish soon was caught up in the game.

No one was paying attention when danger entered the reef. . . .

Suddenly a shark shot like an arrow into the middle of the school. The fish darted in every direction and managed to escape to their hiding place.

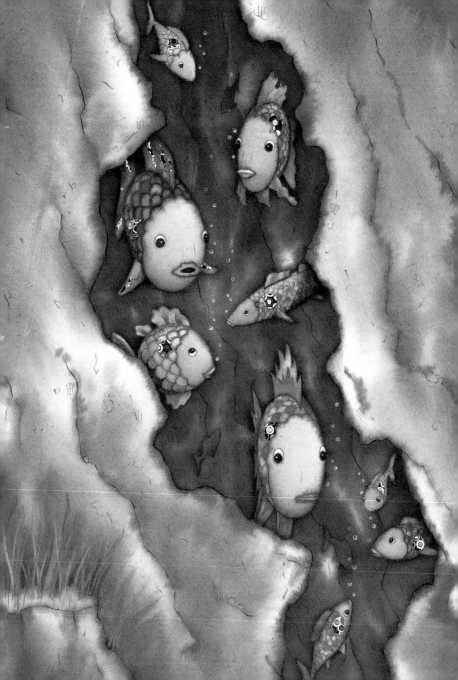

There, in a narrow crack in the reef, the shark could not reach them. They were safe.

But the little striped fish wasn't. Rainbow Fish couldn't keep still, he was so worried.

"What's wrong?" asked the skinny fish.

"It's the little striped fish," said Rainbow Fish. "He's all alone out there. We've got to help him!"

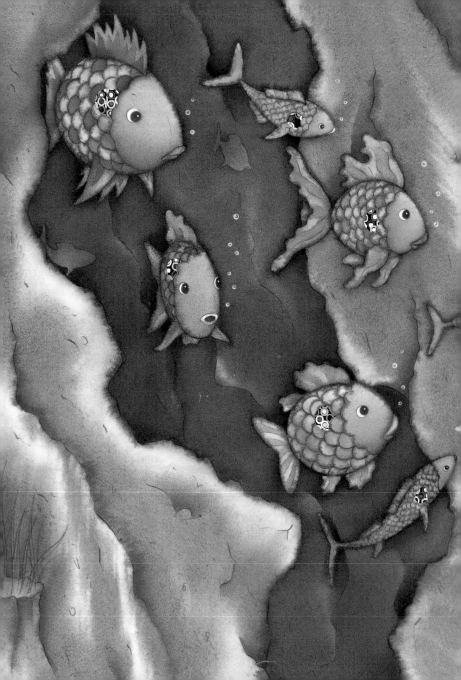

With that, Rainbow Fish left the safety of the
hiding place. "Let's go!" he called.

The other fish trembled with fear, but they
knew what they had to do. They sped out of the
crack after Rainbow Fish.

They soon saw the shark. And there
was the little striped fish, swimming and spinning
away from his jaws. Rainbow Fish could see that
the little fish's strength was failing fast.

"Hurry!" shouted Rainbow Fish, and all the fish
swarmed straight for the shark. This confused the
shark, because usually fish swam *away* from him.
He turned this way and that, snapping right and
left until he was dizzy. The shark almost got the
fish with the jagged fins, but he escaped with
just a few scratches.

Quietly, Rainbow Fish led the little striped fish to safety.

"You were really brave," said the little striped fish. "Thanks for saving my life."

Together, they watched as the exhausted shark gave up and swam away.

When all the fish returned safely to the reef,
they welcomed the little striped fish. "Why don't
you stay and play with us?" Rainbow Fish offered.

"How can I play flash-tag when I don't have a
shiny scale?" asked the little striped fish.

"We can play fin-tag instead!" said the fish with
the jagged fin. "Touch a fin and you're it!"

All the fish cheered, and then they swam off to
play together in the deep blue sea.